D1266818

Flicka, Ricka, Dicka and the LITTLE DOG

MAJ LINDMAN

ALBERT WHITMAN & COMPANY
Morton Grove, Illinois

The Snipp, Snapp, Snurr Books
Snipp, Snapp, Snurr and the Buttered Bread
Snipp, Snapp, Snurr and the Gingerbread
Snipp, Snapp, Snurr and the Red Shoes
Snipp, Snapp, Snurr Learn to Swim

The Flicka, Ricka, Dicka Books
Flicka, Ricka, Dicka and the Little Dog
Flicka, Ricka, Dicka and the New Dotted Dresses
Flicka, Ricka, Dicka and the Three Kittens
Flicka, Ricka, Dicka Bake a Cake

Library of Congress Cataloging-in-Publication Data
Lindman, Maj.
Flicka, Ricka, Dicka and the little dog / Maj Lindman.
p. cm.
Summary: Three little Swedish sisters find a wet and unhappy
dog outside their door on a rainy day, care for him, return
him to his owner—and find him outside again the next day.
ISBN 0-8075-2486-7
[1. Dogs—Fiction. 2. Sisters—Fiction. 3. Sweden—Fiction.] I. Title.
PZ7.L659Fkc 1995   94-37260
[Fic]—dc20   CIP
                                             AC

The text is set in 23' Futura Book
and 12' Bookman Light Italic.

A Flicka, Ricka, Dicka Book

There in a puddle of water sat a little white dog.

Flicka, Ricka, and Dicka have blue eyes and curly golden hair. They always wear dresses that are just alike.

In faraway Sweden there is a pretty yellow house with green shutters and green doors. This is where the three girls live.

One very rainy day, Flicka, Ricka, and Dicka were playing with their dolls. A doll tea party had ended when Flicka said, "Listen. Do you hear that noise?"

Ricka said, "I hear only the rain pounding against the door."

Dicka ran to the window and looked out. There on the step, in a puddle of water, sat a little white dog with one brown ear and one white ear.

The little dog was howling as if to say, "I am wet! I am cold! Won't somebody let me in?"

The three little girls hurried to the door and opened it. "Oh, you poor little dog!" said Flicka.

"You must be very wet and cold," said Ricka. She patted him gently.

"You are probably hungry, too," said Dicka. "Come in."

The little dog stood up and walked slowly into the house, leaving muddy paw marks on the floor.

"Who are you talking to on this rainy afternoon?" asked Mother as she came into the room. Then she saw the open door and the three girls watching the little dog.

The dog shook himself. Drops of water flew in every direction.

Drops of water flew in every direction.

He needs a good hot bath," said Flicka. "He's dirty and cold."

"I'll get the green washtub," said Ricka, "and the soap and the brush."

"I'll get the watering can," said Dicka. "It will work like a shower."

"I'll get a big bath towel to wipe him dry after he is clean," said Flicka.

Soon the little white-and-brown dog stood in the tub of soapy warm water. Ricka scrubbed him gently with the brush, clear to the tip of his white tail.

Dicka stood on the blue chair and poured down a gentle shower of warm water from the green watering can.

Flicka held the big towel. The little dog seemed to understand that they were all good friends.

Soon the little white-and-brown dog stood in the tub.

I do believe you are as clean as soap and water can make you," said Ricka. She helped him out of the tub.

Flicka rubbed him and rubbed him until he was almost dry. Then she sat down in the big yellow rocking chair with the little white-and-brown dog on her lap.

Ricka found a clean wooden box which she partly filled with straw. Over this she laid a cloth that Mother gave her. "This will make a soft bed," she said to Flicka.

Dicka brought a bowl of warm milk. When the little dog had lapped up all he could, he went to sleep in his bed.

"I'm sure you have done all you can for this dog," said Mother. "He is clean and warm. He has taken most of the milk. He will sleep till morning."

Dicka brought a bowl of warm milk.

At bedtime the three girls talked about the little white-and-brown dog. They even went to see if he was sleeping soundly in his warm box.

The next morning Flicka said, "Mother, couldn't we keep the dog? We like him very much."

"I like him, too!" said Mother. "But don't you think such a dog must belong to somebody? Perhaps he is lost. We must look in the morning paper, and if the owner advertises, we must return the dog to him."

Flicka and Mother read the paper. Dicka sat on the floor with her arms around the little dog. Ricka cried softly.

Then Mother read, " 'LOST. A little white dog with one brown ear and one white ear. Answers to the name of Mike. Reward. Tom Carlsson.' "

Flicka and Mother read the paper.

Not many dogs have one brown ear and one white ear," said Mother.

"Mike!" called Flicka. The little dog walked over to her.

"Mike must be his name," said Mother. "I am sure we have Mr. Carlsson's dog. Go and put on your yellow coats and red caps. Then you must take Mike home. Mr. Carlsson owns that big orchard west of town."

Flicka, Ricka, Dicka, and Mike started down the street toward Mr. Carlsson's orchard.

Perhaps Mike was sorry to leave the pretty yellow house. Perhaps he liked to play with the three little girls. As they walked along, Mike sat down with almost every step he took.

Mike sat down with almost every step he took.

Though they pulled and called, Mike did not want to go with them. So the three little girls took turns carrying him.

"I really believe he wants to live with us," said Flicka. "I think he must get lonesome in that big orchard."

Flicka, Ricka, Dicka, and Mike finally reached the orchard, where Mr. Carlsson was busy raking.

"Yes, that's my dog," he said crossly. "He's the watchdog for my orchard. There's his house. You can see his collar and chain fastened to it. Just put his collar on and leave him."

Flicka very gently put the collar on Mike and patted him goodbye. Tears rolled down her cheeks.

Flicka patted him goodbye.

The little girls sadly walked home. "I am sure Mike will be lonely tonight all by himself in that big apple orchard," said Flicka thoughtfully.

"I hope he remembers how happy he was at our house," said Ricka.

But it was Dicka who told Mother all about Mr. Carlsson's needing a watchdog. "Mike is so small for that," she added. Mother agreed with Dicka.

The girls said little at dinner. Each one was thinking of Mike. They said little to each other as they went to bed. Only Flicka said, "Oh dear, I do hope Mike isn't cold."

Early the next morning, soon after sunrise, the girls heard a dog bark. When they opened their window, there was Mike, joyfully wagging his tail and barking, "Good morning!"

There was Mike, joyfully wagging his tail.

How happy the children and Mike were to see each other! Of course, they fed Mike.

Then Mother said thoughtfully, "You know, we really cannot keep what does not belong to us. I am going to take Mike back myself. Do you wish to come with me?"

"But Mother, he won't walk home," said Flicka. "He wants to live with us. We could hardly get him to leave our house yesterday."

"Then I shall carry him," said Mother quietly. "Mike is not our dog."

Then they all started toward the orchard. Mother carried Mike, and the three little girls went sadly along. Flicka walked close beside Mike, holding his front left paw. Ricka patted Mike. Dicka cried a little.

Flicka walked close beside Mike, holding his front left paw.

The girls and Mother talked as they walked along. "I know how you feel," said Mother softly. "I'd like to keep him, too."

Soon they came to the orchard. Mr. Carlsson stood near a ladder, holding two baskets full of apples.

Close by was the doghouse. Next to the doghouse was a large black-and-white dog watching them.

Mr. Carlsson looked at Mother.

"Here's your dog, Mr. Carlsson," began Mother. "He came to our house again."

Before Mother could say more, Mr. Carlsson said crossly, "I have another dog. I bought him yesterday. This is a big orchard, and I think I should have a big watchdog."

Next to the doghouse was a large black-and-white dog.

What about Mike?" asked Dicka. "Won't he have a home anymore?"

"Well," said Mr. Carlsson, "with this new dog, I don't need Mike now. I guess he's too little. Maybe," he went on, "he should have three little girls to play with."

Mother set Mike down carefully. "Do you mean—" she began.

"Mr. Carlsson, may we—" said Flicka.

"Have Mike for our very own?" ended Ricka breathlessly.

"If your mother is willing," he said. "Besides, twice he's found the home that suits him, hasn't he?"

"Yes, he has! Oh, thank you, thank you!" cried the three little girls as Flicka jumped up to kiss him.

Flicka jumped up to kiss him.

Mike seemed to be dancing with joy. Even Mr. Carlsson looked happy now.

"Seems as though children and a little dog always have good times together," he said.

"I want to thank you, too," said Mother, "for giving Mike to the three girls. They love him dearly already."

The three little girls hugged their new pet. Mike was as pleased as he could be. He licked their faces as if to say, "I belong to you now, and I shall live at your house. Won't we have fun playing together!"

Then Flicka, Ricka, Dicka, and Mike ran off through the orchard toward home.

Mother smiled and followed slowly along.

Flicka, Ricka, Dicka, and Mike ran off through the orchard.

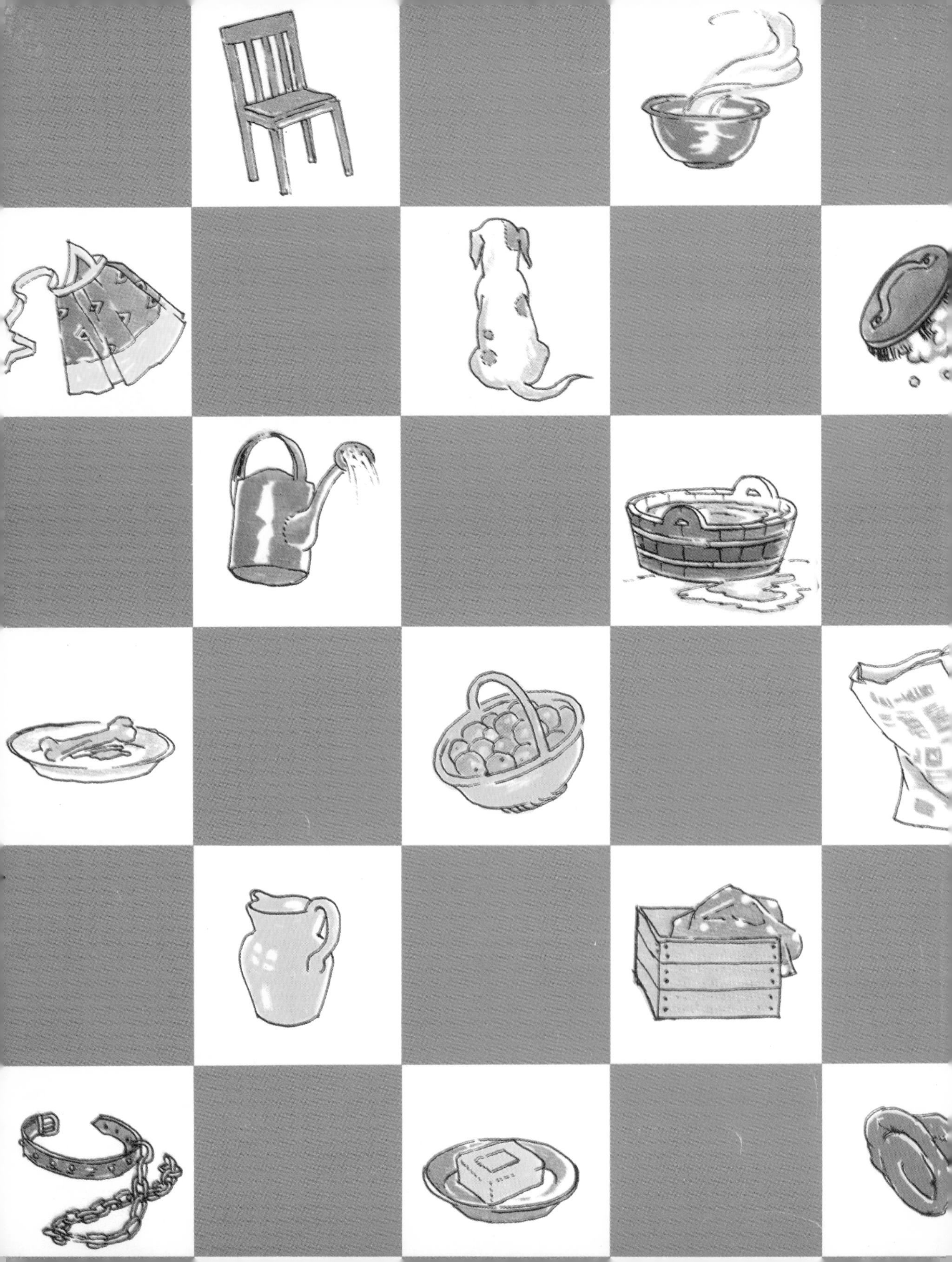